A high five to author and friend Lorie Ann Grover —J. H.
To John and Paul—my two favorite Knuckleheads —M. S.

Text © 2008 by Joan Holub.
Illustrations © 2008 by Michael Slack.

Book design by Sara Gillingham.
The illustrations in this book were rendered digitally.
Manufactured in China.

Library of Congress Cataloging-in-Publication Data
Holub, Joan.
Knuckleheads / by Joan Holub ; illustrations by Michael Slack.
p. cm.
Summary: Presents zany versions of four familiar fairy tales,
retold to feature hands, feet, and other body parts.
ISBN 978-0-8118-5523-5
1. Fairy tales—United States. [1. Fairy tales. 2. Body, Human—Fiction.
3. Humorous stories.] I. Slack, Michael H., 1969- ill. II. Title.
PZ8.H74Knu 2008
[E]—dc22
2008005279

10 9 8 7 6 5 4 3 2 1

Chronicle Books LLC
680 Second Street, San Francisco, California 94107

www.chroniclekids.com

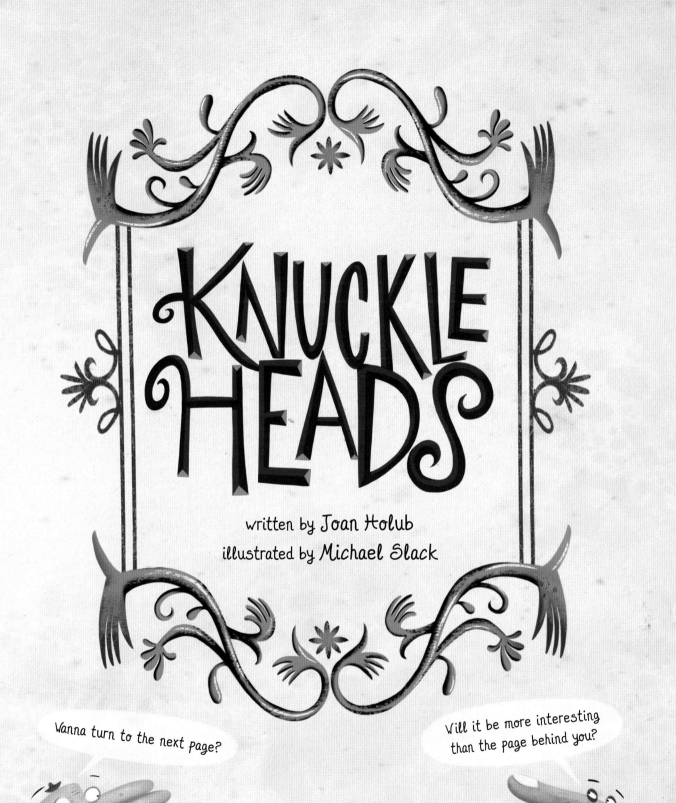

KNUCKLE HEADS

written by Joan Holub

illustrated by Michael Slack

chronicle books · san francisco

Wanna turn to the next page?

Will it be more interesting than the page behind you?

Handsel would only read scratch 'n' sniff books.

He got into fistfights.

POW!

ZONK

And he always forgot to wash his hand after flushing.

"Hey, what's so funny?"

That knucklehead is a handful.

ME

BY: Handsel

HANG NAIL

HANDSEL

INDEX FINGER FILES

PRINCIPAL

Gretel cheated at thumbwrestling.

"You aren't using your finger, too, are you?"

"Who, me? Nuh-uh."

She played shadow-puppets instead of doing her work.

And she always forgot to raise her hand.

"I know! I know! The answer is . . . uh . . ."

She better knuckle down and get to work or it's flunk city for that girl.

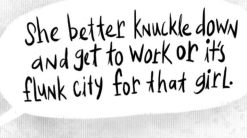

Hands Christian Andersen

A report by: Gretel
Hands wuz a good writur of feery tails like The Toe Queen and The Emperor's New Gloves and...

FLUNK CITY

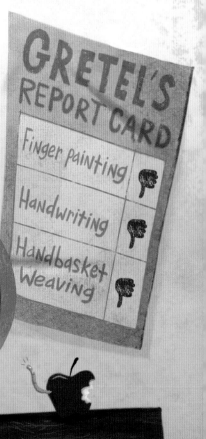

GRETEL'S REPORT CARD

Finger painting	👎
Handwriting	👎
Handbasket Weaving	👎

Things were getting out of hand.
The lunch ladyfinger and
Mr. Hornblower, the substi-toot
music teacher, were out of patience.

"I'm sending a note home
to their parents!"

"I'm fed up
with those two!"

I've had it
with you two
Knuckleheads!

One day, the coach sent them off to play catch.
They went to the outfield and kept on going.
Handsel dropped nail clippings so they could find
their way back to school.

"What's his problem?"

"Athlete's finger,
I'm guessing."

Handsel and Gretel soon found themselves
up to their elbows in problems.
Gretel was quick to point the finger of blame.

"Get lost!"

We're lost and it's all your fault!

NOT IS NOT IS NOT IS NOT IS NOT IS NOT IS NOT IS NOT IS NOT IS IS IS IS NOT IS NOT IS NOT IS NOT IS NOT

INFINITY!

POST NO HANDBILLS

"Say, Buddy, can I thumb a ride?"

"Thumbs down on that idea, Grumpystiltskin."

Suddenly, they bumped
into a house made of
tasty finger food.
They were just about to
start munching, when
they heard a terrible
scraping sound, like
fingernails on a chalkboard.

"Is that witch wearing
brass knuckles?"

"I don't know, but her
mood ring is black!"

Hands off MY
house!

Not
Welcome

The witch put on her evil oven mitt and got out her cooking handbook.

INTO the OVEN, KNUCKLEHEADS!

trubble?

trobule?

Handsel and Gretel were bad readers. But even they knew that spelled trouble. Those two hands began to shake.

Fortunately, before the witch could roast those knuckleheads, Officers Whiteglove and Pointdexter caught the witch red-handed, handcuffed her, and hauled her away.

Unfortunately, she got loose and wound up in another story as you will soon see . . .

He He He
HANDERELLA

There once lived a girl named Handerella,
who worked her fingers to the bone
for her two stepsisters and stepmother.
Those stepsisters didn't lift a finger to help.
(Probably because they were feet.)

How to be a
wicked stepsister
in three easy steps:

1. Step on others' feelings.

2. Step on others' toes.

3. Step on anyone who
gets in your way.

One morning, an invitation arrived from the handsome Finger Prints. The stepsisters kicked up their heels and jumped for joy.

Her stepmother made Handerella give them pedicures. Then they all three hotfooted it outta there . . .

. . . leaving Handerella behind.

So long Handerella. We're stepping out! Don't you just love my new open-toed sandals?

Shake a leg, girls. It's getting late.

I hope the Prints doesn't notice my hammer toe.

Luckily, the Fickle-Finger-of-Fate Fairy flew in.

You need a manicure big time, Handerella. But no time for a total makeover. Just slip this evening glove on. And this sparkly ring, too.

Meanwhile, the stepsisters were having a ball.
But things turned to toe jam when Handerella showed up.
Soon the stepsisters were feeling like two left feet.

Handerella and the Finger Prints
danced hand in hand.
They spoke the same language.
All the signs were there.

It was true love.

clang! *clang!*
clang! *clang!* *clang!*
clang! *clang!* *clang!*
clang! *clang!* *clang!*
clang! *clang!* *clang!*

The royal wristwatch struck 12,
so Handerella hurried home.
Her evening glove turned into a
rubber dishwashing glove.
Her dazzling ring slipped through
her fingers and rolled away.

The next day, the Finger Prints gave Handerella's doorbell a ring.

If this ring fits, I will marry you.

Goody. I've always wanted to be a wedding bell.

The ring didn't fit her doorbell, so he tried it on the stepsisters.

WOW! Is that toe-paz?

That's odd. I don't remember Handerella having athlete's foot.

I'm a size 6. HONEST! Get me some lotion. I'll slide that ring on somehow.

"She couldn't get that ring on with a shoehorn!"

BiGFoot Lotion

When the ring didn't fit the stepsisters, they got so hoppin' mad, that they drop-kicked it.

It flew to Handerella and slid right on her finger.

?

The Finger Prints asked Handerella
for her hand in marriage.
She gave him a thumbs up
and waved good-bye
to her stepfamily.
But the stepsisters didn't
admit de-feet gracefully.

"Handsome, my foot.
He's not so buff."

"That Prints is
so under her thumb."

HEY LOOK!
That Witch — I
mean Stepmother —
is sneaking into
another story.

THUMBELINA

Thumbelina was tiny.

She was no bigger than a walnut,
or maybe a thimble, or kind of
like a stick of gum, but a little more
the size of a thread spool, only sort of
caterpillaristically inclined, but not
fuzzy or anything . . .

Okay, we get it.
She was one
short finger.

Thumbelina was made by a witch,
stolen by a toad, and
almost married to a mole.
Finally, a bird carried her away
to a flower, where she got wings
and lived happily ever after.

Thumbelina was short. And so is her story.

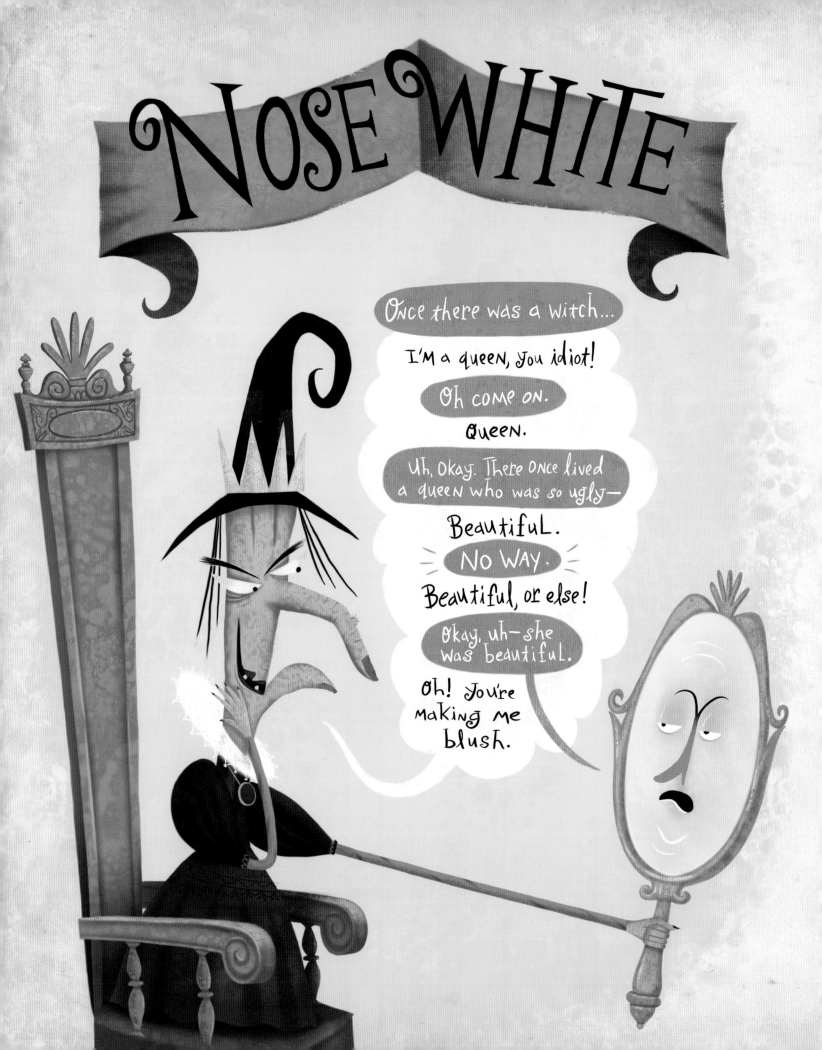

The queen couldn't stand playing secondhand fiddle to anyone. She quickly hired a handyman and told him:

Take that snotty Nose White into the forest and give her a punch in the schnozz!

THIS WAY TO THE PALMTREE FOREST

But the hired hand was a peaceful man.

He took Nose White into the forest and let her go.

DANGER
BLOCKED NASAL PASSAGES
AHEAD

She nosed around the forest until she met a one-hand band.
Pinky, Ringo, Snappy, Picker, and Thumbkin dug her nasal sound
and asked her to join them. Turns out, they were
friends she could count on (at least up to five).

Soon, Nose White's life
was smelling like a rose.

But the next day, the Queen asked her mirror, "Who's the most beautiful now?"

UPON reflection, it's still... Nose White!

When she heard that, the Queen snapped.

Looks like I'll have to take matters into my own hand and put a stop to this NONSENSE myself!

The Queen grabbed some dandelions and hand-delivered them to Nose White.

Nose White took one sniff.

She sneezed. She wheezed. Then she took a nose dive. She was completely stopped up.

Of all the underhanded tricks!

That Queen sure gave her a nose job.

Along came a handsome prince.

He offered Nose White
a handkerchief.
(That came in handy!)

She blew and blew and blew.

When Nose White finally stopped, she wasn't stopped up anymore. She and the prince wound up on an island somewhere in the Finger Lakes.

Auntie EM!

Wow! You really blew me away with your charm.

Oh, it was nothing. I'm just glad our story has a happy ending.

"Think that witch is gone for good? Think again!"

Coming soon! Watch for these books starring the hand-witch:

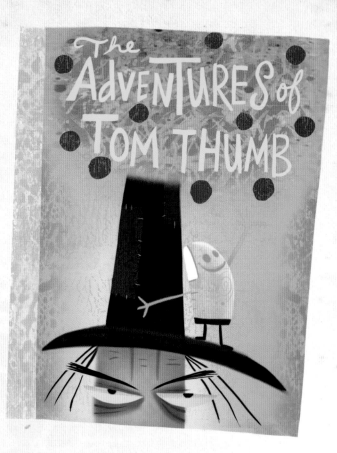

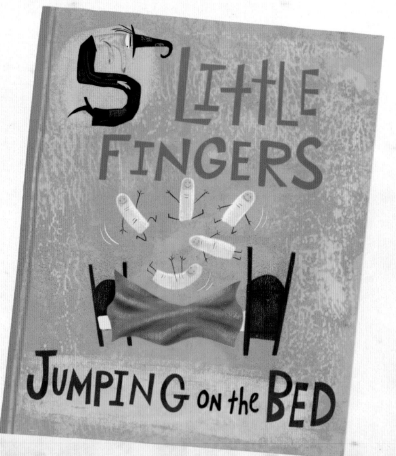

"That looks like fun!"

HEEL THY SELF

No AuToGRAPHS!

Here's what reviewers whose palms have been greased have to say about *Knuckleheads*:

"Handtastic!" — *High Five Magazine*

"It grew on me." — *The Green Thumb Gazette*

"Picked it up, dropped it, picked it up, dropped it."
— *The Bigger, Better Butterfingers Bureau*

"Touching." — *The New York Braille-y News*

"We see a great future for the witch character.
We see a window of opportunity. And a stepstool
named Rapunzel?" — *The Palm Reader's Digest*

"An even-handed storytelling." — *The Ten Finger Times*

The End